WHO-2

THE ENFORCEMENT OF YOUTH ESPIONAGE

JANUSHI RAICHURA

Contents

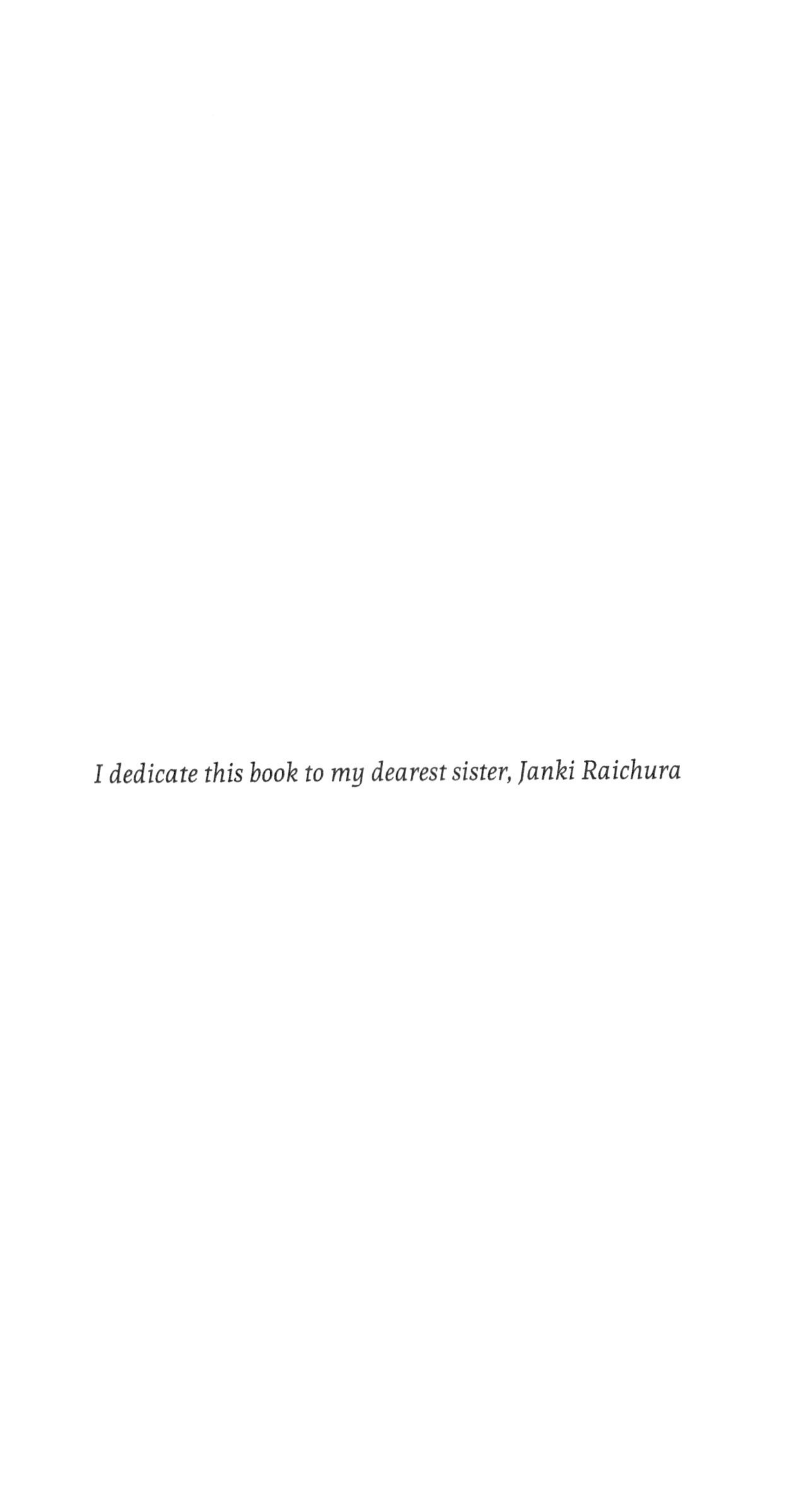

I dedicate this book to my dearest sister, Janki Raichura

1

Liabilities

Antsiyanah walked to the interrogation room. She sat on the other side of the glass and watched as Carol questioned Bellora. Enif stood beside her, looking highly annoyed. From the look on Carol's face, the interrogation wasn't going well. Bellora was in tears and for once, Lyric felt sympathetic towards her, but she quickly composed her emotions. It was either her or Bellora on the chair.

Her nose almost touched the glass and she could feel Enif's eyes on her, but she didn't bother looking back, she knew he wanted to ask or tell her something.

"Lyric," he started. *Here it goes.* She thought.

"Yes?" She asked sweetly, batting her lashes.

"I don't believe that Bellora did this."

"What makes you think she didn't?" she questioned.

"For starters, she's isn't saying anything. All she has done is cry. Maybe we have got the wrong person."

"Enif, seriously?" she exclaimed rolling her eyes. "Look, she could be acting for all we know. Besides, give her one good reason to run after you know, revealing her honey-blond hair! Which, we have no idea why she even coloured! Oh, wait, I know. To hide the fact that she is Mrs

Anonymous." He didn't reply, so she went on. "I know you have always had a soft for her. She has been so nice and sweet, but Enif, we might have a world-class criminal right now, right here. We can't disregard that." She spoke softly, trying to soothe him and make him believe that Bellora was at fault there. Carol chose that moment to come out of the room to them.

"She's saying nothing. Enif, can I have a word in private?" The both of them excused themselves and went inside another cabin to talk. Lyric, more precisely Antsiyanah, worked at a European secret agency, E.Y.E, Enforcement of Youth Espionage in the branch Operations Intelligence Wing (OIW). She was a forensic doctor there. Antsiyanah wasn't Lyric, she was pretending to be Lyric. In reality, she was the world-class criminal the whole world was looking for. Mrs Anonymous. Antsiyanah had a sharp brain, so after she and her friend Alejandro ran away from their orphanage, she joined medical, while Alejandro joined the forces. Faster than humanly possible, Antsiyanah gained a PhD in forensics, along with the thieveries she and Alex (Alejandro) used to do. Living with him, she even got training in physical combat. The both of them got married when they were just nineteen, and had a daughter named Amara. Amara was really smart for her age. She was barely six, but she was great with technology. She put trackers and cameras on everything. That was her idea of fun. Adelmo, Antsiyanah's best friend, used to take care of Amara. They had an orphanage of their own, a quite different orphanage, where children were taught stuff other than studies. Not thievery, no. They were given combat training, strategizing courses, and other kinds of pieces of training that would help them in the real world. Most of the kids there were geniuses, much like Amara. About three years ago, Alex had died, or so everyone believed. He was running from someone and had pretended to die. Recently, he had made a very dramatic entrance. But everything had changed. Antsiyanah had married Clifford Courteney, one of the richest and nicest persons in France. So, she and Alex had been distant. He had almost uncovered her identity, but then he had helped her frame Bellora and capture her. The whole of France was now on the lookout for him, and she hadn't seen him for a while, but she wasn't worried; she knew he was more than capable of taking care of himself.

She knew why he was staying away. He couldn't face Amara. They had met once, but at that time, he had a knife under Antsiyanah's throat and was threatening to kill her. That hadn't made a great impression on Amara, and now, Amara would call Antsiyanah every night, just to make sure she was okay. Once Antsiyanah was with Alex when Amara had called and Amara had called Alex a 'murderer' and had told Antsiyanah to be careful. Alex had heard it, and he was deeply hurt, and that was also the last time Antsiyanah had seen Alex.

As if on cue, her phone rang. She picked it up and heard a very excited voice from the other line, "Is this Ms Lyric Bouvier?"

"Yes. Who is this?"

"It's the florist, from down the street, ma'am. Ma'am, I have your sunset orange daffodils ready, please collect them." She knew the voice, it was Alex. And he was giving her a coded message.

"Sure." She cut the phone. It was their anniversary, and he wanted her to come by the Eiffel Tower, the symbol of love, at dusk.

Could he be more obvious? She thought. She put her phone in her purse and turned around just in time to see Enif and

Carol walk out of the cabin.

"What was that about?" Antsiyanah asked Enif who was dabbing his handkerchief at the sweat trickling down his temples.

"I can't tell you. It's a 'muscle secret'." The combat spies of the agency and doctors and engineers had a thing. The 'muscle secret' was something to be kept only between the combat spies while the 'brain secret' was to be kept only between the doctors and engineers. "Lyric, don't you have somewhere to be?"

"I completed my assignment an hour ago, that's why I came here."

"Well, you can't just *come here*."

"Sure I can. I am in the case"

"No, you aren't. Not anymore."

"You are removing me?"

"We are just getting rid of all the liabilities."

"Excuse me? Are you calling me a liability?" she asked feigning drama and anger.

"It was the decision of the whole team. Minimize the number, minimize the chances of defeat." Enif replied coldly. There was something Carol had told him. Something was wrong about this all.

"Fine! I'll get rid of myself!" she grabbed her purse, pushed the door out open, and slapped it shut behind her loudly, and dramatically.

2
Guilt Trip

"Alejandro, what do you want?" she asked standing against the railing of the tower.

"I wanted to talk to you. There's something you should know."

"Get to it!" she yelled irritably.

"I know you're mad at me...And I am very sorry for what I did. That was stupid and immature and impulsive of me."

"What are you apologizing for? Knife under my throat?"

"That too. But mainly for abandoning you and Amara."

"I get why you did it. But you had no right to make that decision. You had no right to choose for me or Amara."

"Can we just put it behind us?"

"Don't you get it? We can't! We can't just resume our life as nothing had happened. I have a life here now, and so does Amara. If I leave now, they're going to doubt me."

"They already are doubting you. That's why they took you off the case. Because they think you are somehow involved in all this."

"What? But how did they find out?"

"I don't know. I am guessing the honey-blonde hair and all your made-up past drama. I have sources in your agency, they informed me."

"Dammit! I thought the bullets and everything would convince them that I was the last person who could be her!"

"I am guessing that just added to their suspicion. What are the loose ends, An?"

"Mr Bakers, Lyric's family, orphanage records. But none of the above confirms that I am Mrs Anonymous."

"There is nothing you missed out, An? Are you a hundred per cent sure of that?"

"No, Alejandro, I am not a hundred person sure of that. I have my doubts. But if they are smart enough, they can just join the dots, A. The theft at mom's place was a big giveaway." Lady Valarie had finally let Lyric call her 'mom'. As much as Lyric was happy about it, the fact that none of that was permanent hurt her a lot.

"Mom? Right, Lady Valarie. Look, I am sorry about that thievery."

"I guess today's the day when you finally apologize for a billion things you shouldn't have done but you still did. You can apologize later; we need to focus on the problems right now."

"Are they smart enough to connect the dots?"

"We are talking about the biggest European spy agency here. Of course, they are smart enough. And Bellora might be a bit of an issue. She might know about the fact that I already knew she had blonde hair which she had dyed."

"Want me to take care of her?" She knew it was his way of saying, 'Want me to kill her?' He didn't like mentioning murders openly, so he said it in another way.

"It will draw too much suspicion. We'll just be confirming their doubts."

"What if someone else confessed that she is Mrs Anonymous?"

"That could work. But who would do that?"

"We just need the right bribe and threat and a blonde, obviously."

"What if it's someone from the team? That will make it more convincible."

"Someone blond in it?"

"Leighton's there. She's in the 'muscle' squad. She is arrogant, strong, smart. But if they check her past records…"

"I'll get rid of them. Anything around the time of theft on her. I'll ask my sources to remove or tamper them from your E.Y.E. An, be very careful. One mistake and you'll be dead."

"I know, A, I know. But I have never made a mistake, to this day. I am pretty sure I'll stick to that perfection till I am dead."

"Which is not anytime soon," Alex stated as a matter-of-factly.

"Yeah, it's so not anytime soon. It's not like I am dying or anything." Lyric replied awkwardly. Alex eyed her suspiciously but then turned away.

"See you later, Antsiyanah," she left without a word. Clifford was waiting for her at her home. It seemed as though he had been waiting for a long time cause he looked very impatient.

"Fifteen missed calls, Lyric. And a dozen messages! Enif told me you left around two!"

"I needed to take a beat." She replied quietly.

"You could've answered a call, or left a message. For once, why can't you be a little responsible sometimes, Lyric?" he shouted, getting up.

"Oh, so, even you think I am a liability? Why does everyone think I am not responsible?" Lyric shouted back, tears coming out of her eyes. She wasn't crying because she was brought out by the team. She was crying because she wanted to put all of this behind her. She wanted the past two and a half years to be erased from existence. She wanted to pick up from where they had left off before things went south. Everything was so great. Quiet, fun, thrilling. She didn't realize when Cliff had wrapped his arm around her and had walked her to the couch, where she cried her eyes out, with her head pressed against his chest and him running his hand through her hair. She was so upset, so fed up, so tired, that the tears didn't stop. She wanted to be with Amara and Alex. And here she was, married to a rich man, and her life crumbling down. Clifford kissed her head, which added more to her sorrow. She felt guilty for playing with his feelings, but there was nothing else she could do. She never thought she would feel guilty for it, but now she did. She didn't expect him to be so nice. She thought he would be mean, and that guilt would never be an issue. Things were different now. He had turned out to be the most understanding person ever. She didn't deserve it. None of it. Not his warmth, kindness, friendliness. None of it. She didn't realize when she fell asleep in his arms.

3

Pure

Cliff looked down at Lyric, who was sleeping peacefully in his arms. He couldn't believe what Enif had told him. It wasn't possible. He refused to believe it all. She was an angel incarnate, not anything Enif had told him. He stroked her hair and placed a kiss on her forehead. His hands wandered to where she was shot. He rolled up her top to get a look at it. She had healed up well, but still, as his fingers brushed against her cold skin, she winced in her sleep. He immediately rolled her top back down and ran a hand through her hair.

"Cliff…" she whispered. He cursed at himself for waking her up.

"Sorry I-" he started but she went on.

"I am so sorry, Cliff." She muttered, and he realized she was talking in her sleep. He turned quiet. He wanted to know what she was apologizing for. "I am sorry. I shouldn't have done it. I…" her voice drowned down, and she fell back asleep.

He carried her to their room and put her on the bed. He covered her with blankets and tucked her in. He went to check Lyric's phone. There was a call earlier from an unknown number that Lyric had received. Following Enif's instructions, he called back.

"Hello…" he heard a man greet seriously.

"Who's this?" there was a silence for a brief moment before the man replied.

"I am the florist from down the street." The man's voice turned cheerful.

"Why did you call?"

"Mrs Courteney wanted daffodils." His eyes met the bouquet of daffodils on the table.

"Where is your shop?"

"I move about all of the Paris."

"Can we meet?"

"Is there a specific flower you would like, sir?"

"Yes. Um…do you have lilies?"

"Yes sir. I'll bring them to your house. Can you please give me your address?" Cliff gave him his address. "Thank you, sir. I'll be there, the first thing tomorrow morning." The line went silent and Cliff opened Lyric's location history to check where she was. Her location was off, so her history was blank. No better time to turn it on. He put her phone away.

He had to wait for a couple of hours for Lyric to get up, during which he went through his work. Lyric came out of their room yawning childishly. And the way she looked with her hair messy and her eyes dizzy, you would never believe a thing against her.

"'Morning, Cliff!"

"It's night…"

"Huh…guess I slept for a long time!" she marked sleepily, stretching 'long'. "Wonder why I want to sleep more…"

"Coffee?"

"Hell no. I'll be a zombie the whole night."

"You look really pretty..." he complimented, entwining his hand with hers.

"You don't call me that when I get dressed up for parties. And you're calling me that now when I have a bird's nest for hair."

"You look like yourself right now."

"Are you calling me messy?" she asked playfully, folding her hands.

"I am calling you pure..." she turned a light shade of pink and raised her hands childishly for a hug. Cliff hugged her and walked her to bed. He put her to sleep, and later, after wrapping up all his work, fell asleep himself.

Lyric was up when he woke up. She was on the breakfast table in their yard, where the maid was pouring her coffee. She was dressed up in fresh clothes and was reading a newspaper. He got ready himself before joining her. She looked frustrated, but as he approached her frustration was replaced by a smile and she said, "Did I ever tell you how good you look in a suit?"

"Hmm...must've forgotten to mention..." he replied, taking a seat across her. She put away the newspaper and took a sip of her untouched coffee. "Shouldn't you be at work?"

"I talked to Sir Patrick, he advised me some rest from all the Mrs Anonymous drama."

"So you're not going to work for a few days?"

"Nuh-uh. Not giving up that easily. I convinced Sir Patrick to put me on another case. Do you know there is a serial killer on a killing spree in Italy? And did you know that there might be a terrorist attack at the president's meeting next month at Lille?" Cliff shook his head. "Well, there it is. But apparently, there are enough 'brains' there in O.I.W and C.H.R.I.S.T working on those cases." C.H.R.I.S.T stood for Critical Hustle and Research for Intelligence and Subtotal Terrorism. "So, I have to solve the mystery of the lost dog of Mrs Pumpkin! I think that's her name..."

"That's insulting! You're the smartest in your department!"

"Not smart enough, obviously..."

"Patrick wants you to have a break, Lyric. That's all. What do you say to going to Los Angeles?"

Shock reflected on Lyric's face. She was speechless for a moment, but then she composed herself. "I can't go there! You know I can't."

"Mrs Anonymous already knows you are alive-"

"It's dangerous for my family!"

"What about me? Is it not dangerous for me?"

"You want me to move away? Okay, I'll move away!"

"That's not what I mean, Lyric, much less what I want! I am just saying that you can meet your friends and family now. You don't have to stay away from them!"

"Cliff, even I want to meet them! But I just can't, Cliff. You know I can't!"

"Vegas?"

"A little over the top, don't you think?"

"New York?"

"Too busy..."

"San Francisco?"

"Too sunny..."

"Where do you want to go then?"

"Let's just stay here..." He didn't pressure her. He had to leave for an urgent meeting but was reluctant to leave Lyric alone. Lucky for him, she had to leave to find Mrs Pumpkin's 'dog'. He felt pity for her. She had the brain of a genius but was forced to work on cases below her level. It was her passion, they had enough money for generations below them to live lavishly. But they both loved their work and seeing her work on stupid things upset him.

Between all of it, he had forgotten about the florist. Just as he was about to leave, he saw a cart pull up in front of their gate. He permitted the guard to allow the man in with his cart. Lyric was surprised to see a whole cart filled with flowers. The man pulled his cart on the garden in front of Lyric, just like Cliff directed him.

"I thought you might want some flowers to cheer you up. I got you lilies, your favourite."

"Aw, Cliff, thank you…"

"I have to go, I am getting late. Pick up the bouquet of your choice…" Lyric nodded beaming.

4

Daffodils and Lilies

"Why did Clifford call me?" Alex asked as soon as Cliff left. Antsiyanah looked around to be sure no one was there before replying.

"What are you doing here?"

"Clifford called me yesterday and asked me why I had called you. Then he asked me to bring you lilies."

"Enif must've told him to keep an eye on me..."

"I thought you liked daffodils..."

"My preferences have changed."

"I can see that. But so have his, An."

"What do you mean?"

"Clifford doesn't have a meeting today. He's lying to you about his whereabouts."

"Where is he going then?"

"Find out yourself. I hardly think you'll like the answer." Alex handed her a bouquet before pulling the cart out of the house. He had put in an effort for this act. Lucky for them, Cliff didn't doubt him one bit. Now, Lyric was worried about where Cliff was. She knew it wasn't something related to her cover, or Alex would've been more serious.

She called the man Cliff had told her he had a meeting with. "Good morning, Lord Frankston. I am Lyric Courteney, Clifford's wife. Is he there with you, Lord?"

"Oh, Lady Courteney, I have heard a lot about you. Clifford isn't here, no, we met yesterday though for a meeting. Is everything okay?"

"Yes, I forgot where Clifford had his meeting today. His phone's coming switched off. It's nothing serious, I am sure he's okay."

"Let's pray so. Feel free to call me, Lady, in case any emergency arises."

"Thank you, Lord Frankston."

"Anytime..." Lyric wanted to throw the phone but controlled herself. She had a tracker on his phone, which she used to find him. She called Sir Patrick to inform him that she would be taking a day off. She tracked him down, and she did not like where he was.

"Where were you?" she asked as soon as he got back, her face red from crying.

"Lyric, why are you crying?" he asked apprehensively, taking off his blazer and putting it on a chair.

"Where were you?"

"I told you, I had a meeting with Mr Frankston."

"Liar! I called him. He said you had a meeting yesterday. Or did you have a meeting at Soliel Calistèe de la Roche's house?"

"How-"

"Why did you lie to me, Cliff?"

He gave a small smile before hugging her. "You trust me?" she nodded on his shoulder. "Then get ready for a date night. I'll tell you, more like, show you over dinner."

She didn't argue. She got ready as quietly as possible, not to attract Cliff's attention with her crying. But she believed him, the smile he gave told her that it was something for her. And she felt horrible for doubting him.

They drove to a rooftop restaurant, and behind them, the chauffeur carried something huge wrapped in an expensive paper. From the dimensions, Antsiyanah could tell it was a painting, most likely for her. She felt horrible for doubting his whereabouts, of course, he was bringing something for her, he always did. Soliel Calistèe de la Roche was a famous painter and was from a royal family.

"This must've cost a lot, Cliff. I know Soliel only deals in millions!"

"It didn't cost me anything, An. Soliel is an old childhood friend, she did it for free because I helped her family a lot when they got bankrupt. And even if it did cost me much, you didn't have to worry about it, okay? Your husband owns about half of France, he has enough money to buy his wife a painting."

"Thanks, Cliff, this means a lot to me."

"I know, Lyric, I know." He drove them back home. They didn't sleep much that night; they first watched some movies and then talked until Cliff fell asleep. Lyric couldn't sleep, so she walked out to their garden to stare at the sky. She was thinking about Alejandro and was wondering why he had made her doubt Cliff. She knew he knew why he was at Soliel Roche's house, and she wondered why he had lied to her.

"Hello, Lyric," She felt someone familiar creep up behind her.

"It's Antsiyanah to you!" she replied without turning back. She knew the voice too well. "It's dangerous for you to come here!"

"I know how to hide, An."

"Why did you lie when you knew why he wasn't where he told me he would be?"

"I just wanted to know for sure."

"Wanted to know what, A?"

"You love him don't you, An? You were hurt, and you don't do hurt An. You get back at people, you don't confront them to confirm it, but you trusted him, An, that's why you confronted him. I was expecting you to burn his house down, empty all his accounts; but you just broke down. You love him!"

"No-"

"He called you 'An' tonight! He knows, doesn't he?" Antsiyanah suddenly felt tired. She didn't want to have this conversation, but she was left with no choice but to continue this conversation.

"I told him before we got married when he proposed. He knows I am not Lyric, and he knows about the orphanage and everything. He just doesn't know that I am Mrs Anonymous. He even knows about Amara-"

"He-what? You told him about Amara? Are you out of your mind?"

"I trust him, Alex-"

"I don't even know where Amara lives, and he knows of her existence? I am her father!"

"And I see how well you've been looking after your responsibilities as a father!"

"You didn't give me a chance!"

"I-I am sorry, Alex. I am so sorry for all of this, I didn't mean for this to happen, I thought you died!"

"I am sorry too,"

"For what?" She should've seen it coming, as she felt a handkerchief on her mouth, covering her nose, and a familiar smell; and she blacked out.

5

Rusty

When she woke up, she was in an empty hospital ward, on a hospital bed, cuffed to the bed. She groaned as the light hit her eyes. She tried to wriggle free but failed miserably.

"Good you're up, I was starting to get worried!" She knew that he wasn't worried at all. "My sweet Antsiyanah, I would never do anything to harm you!" she noticed the IVs connected to her arms. Her throat felt sore, and her breathing came harder than usual.

"What did you do to me?"

"Nothing you need to worry about!"

"Let me go!" Tears fell from her eyes, and his expression turned grim.

"I am not going to hurt you, An, at least trust me that much!"

She didn't complain, she trusted him not to kill her.

"Has Clifford ever met Amara?"

"They've met a couple of times," She lied looking away. Clifford and Amara were very close, and they had met a lot more than a couple of times.

"Pick one," he pulled out two different kinds of knives and showed them to her.

"I thought you said you wouldn't hurt me!"

"These aren't for you!"

"Please don't hurt Cliff. You said you wouldn't hurt me, and hurting Cliff would be emotionally hurting me!"

"You always had a way with words," he stabbed the table with them and Antsiyanah winced. "What's wrong with you? Where's the fun Antsiyanah who would've given back a snarky response?"

"I've changed!"

"It's not just a tiny change, you've become a completely different person, An! And look at stupid me, who still loves you!"

"Then why are you doing this?"

"To try to bring the fun Antsiyanah back," he took her phone from the pocket of her clothes which were lying in a corner since she was in a hospital gown. He called someone, and Antsiyanah hoped it wouldn't go as bad as she thought it would go. "Adelmo, hey, long time no see, buddy!" he paused as Adelmo responded on the phone. "She's right here. Here in the sense, in an abandoned yet fully functional hospital right on the outskirts of Paris. Come here and save your 'very capable of saving herself' damsel. And oh, don't forget to bring Amara with you." He cut the phone and sat beside Antsiyanah. "You feeling okay?" he asked softly.

"What did you do?" she questioned back in the same quiet tone.

"Remember that stone I stole from your husband? I put that in your throat. Remember you once told me there was a tiny place in our throat, big enough to fit a diamond. Well, I filled it with that diamond."

"Take it out!" she demanded indignantly, but he scoffed in response. "I mean it, take it out!"

"Why should I?"

"Because I am asking you to. Does that mean nothing to you?" he didn't reply. "My throat hurts…"

"I'll call a doctor!" As soon as he got out of the door, she moved her legs to draw the table which had the knives closer to her. She pulled out the IVs from her hands and grabbed the knife. She cut the wood of the bed to which her right hand was cuffed to and then did the same with the wood to which her left hand was cuffed to.

Alex must've heard the commotion, because the next second, he got inside the room.

"That's my girl!" he complimented, raising his hands in a surrender gesture.

"I am going back home!" She got past him and was almost outside the door, when he grabbed his wrist, pulled her back, and pinned her hand carrying the knife behind her back.

"Not so soon. You've grown rusty, An, I am disappointed!"

"And I don't care!"

"What home do you want to go to? To your fake husband who does not know you are a world-class criminal and have murdered innocents for self-preservation?"

"None of them were innocents!"

"Then why haven't you told him yet?"

"You know what, I should, and I will. Just let me go back to him!"

"Not yet. Now sit down like a good girl and wait for Adelmo and Amara with me. You'll go after I see my daughter." Antsiyanah didn't argue. She quietly sat back down. "And don't try anything please, An. I seriously don't want this to get messy."

"You kidnapped me, then put my husband's most prized possession in my throat and now, you are telling me that you don't want this to get messy?" he sat beside her and took her hand reassuringly as if trying to prove that he didn't want this to get messy. Antsiyanah believed him, she knew he didn't want it to get worse; she knew he didn't want *them* to get worse.

They both sat silently for a while, neither of them making a sound. Antsiyanah felt dizzy, and she wanted to sleep; probably it was because she had gone through some surgery or something, or probably it was because she hadn't had any actual sleep in a while; she wasn't sure which one of them was the cause.

She heard footsteps approach her and she turned around to find Amara and Adelmo running towards her.

"Are you okay, mommy?" she asked Antsiyanah, who forced a smile to assure her daughter, who looked like she had been crying.

"Alejandro, heard you were alive!" Adelmo greeted, smiling. Adelmo and Alejandro were best friends, but ever since Alejandro had pretended to die, they hadn't met. Antsiyanah was glad to see that the warmth between the two of them was still there, and she hoped it would linger.

"Heard you looked after my wife and daughter. Thanks, man,"

"No worries. Now, Cliff and Enif are on the lookout for her, she needs to go back or there will be a lot of suspicions."

"Don't worry about that. Hey, Amara," he got down on his knees to match Amara's height. "How are you?"

"What did you do to my mother? Why is she so upset?"

6

Maniac

"I am not upset, darling, I am good," Antsiyanah explained softly and Alejandro looked at her gratefully.

"I am Alejandro," he offered his hand which she quietly shook.

"I am Amara." She smiled at him, and Antsiyanah sighed in relief.

This is going considerably well. She thought and crouched beside Alejandro, to make both him and Amara more comfortable.

"So, what do you like to do, Amara?" he asked conversationally, folding his legs and Amara did the same.

"Most of the time I like indulging in fighting and hacking. Adelmo and mom teach me and give me challenges. I also like playing with the other kids."

Antsiyanah watched as Alejandro made conversation, as he made Amara laugh. Antsiyanah didn't interrupt them, she just sat there. Every once in a while, Alejandro would look over at her, silently asking for her approval while raising a conversation, and she would give a slight nod and an overjoyed smile.

She remembered a time when things used to be normal; normal for them. Until Lyric Bouvier ruined their lives. She recounted her old memories. Amara didn't remember him clearly; she was barely three back then. But she knew Alejandro remembered it all too well. She was enjoying everything until she felt an ache in her chest. She looked up at Adelmo before she started coughing violently. Her lungs were compressed, and she was having trouble breathing.

"Where's her purse?" Adelmo asked furiously.

"What's wrong?" Alejandro questioned back, pointing at her white purse laid neatly beside her clothes. Adelmo pulled out her medicines from her purse and handed them to her with a glass of water. He helped her take them and then turned to Alejandro. "Antsiyanah, what's wrong?"

She shook her head in response, but couldn't answer. Amara doesn't say anything, she is more used to this, she just hugs Antsiyanah to give her comfort.

"I am good, baby," she soothed Amara, trying to smile at her, but even Amara knew something was wrong. She turned to Alejandro, who she hadn't seen look more worried than he did at that moment. She waved her hand, signalling him to brush it off, which he did. "Adelmo, Amara, you should get going."

"Amara isn't going anywhere!" Alejandro said sharply.

"Yes, she is. She's going-"

"With me. I am her father."

"Alex, we've been over this. She isn't comfortable around strangers-"

"I am sorry, what? Did you just call me a stranger?" he gently took Amara's hand, and Antsiyanah looked at him dangerously, knowing what he was going to do. He pulled Amara into his lap, faster than light, and had a knife under her throat the next second. Amara yelped, and Antsiyanah reached out a hand to pull Amara back but Alejandro stopped her. "You don't want her dead, do you?"

"You wouldn't hurt her, she's your daughter!"

"You know how much of a maniac I am, Antsiyanah. Want me to prove it?" Amara tried to push the knife away, but being a kid, she didn't know pushing the sharp side of the blade would only cause her more pain. Blood trickled down her fingers and Antsiyanah winced. She didn't trust Alejandro, she knew he would do anything to get what he wanted. He didn't notice Amara's blood. He got up and walked out of the door, with Amara with him.

Adelmo looked at her, not sure if what he had just seen was true or not. She got up, knowing how much sense it all made. It was all a part of his plan. "You stay here, I'll make sure Enif finds you. I'll cuff you to the bed again." She nodded and let him do it. He left and Antsiyanah just stared outside the window, waiting for someone to find her.

About an hour or two later, she heard sirens. She tried to peep outside the window, but it was too far away. Soon, the whole hospital was crowded with the police. Enif ran up to her and picked the lock of her cuffs. He carefully pulled her out of the ward, and as she passed other rooms, she saw a bunch of doctors lying dead. She felt guilty, and turned away, trying to stop the tears forming in her eyes from falling.

Enif held her protectively, just like always. Enif was in his early fifties, but for someone that old, he was pretty strong and smart. Sometimes, he treated her like she was his daughter.

He navigated her through all the chaos and mayhem. Some cops approached her, but Enif signalled them to stay back. He took her right to his car, and carefully seated her inside. She tried her best to not break into tears, and it worked...until Enif asked her to tell him what was wrong.

She knew she was going to break, he daughter was taken away from her, but she couldn't tell him that. She just shook her head and he didn't question her any further. Tears threatened to fall, but she controlled herself; she knew if she let even one tear fall, more would soon follow.

Enif drove her back home. It was the protocol to take a spy for interrogation after finding them in such a situation, but Enif was kind enough to first take her back home because he knew she was emotionally unstable at the moment. She knew how much trouble he could get in for that, and was grateful towards him for that.

He led her into her and Cliff's house, through the hallways to Cliff. Cliff was in their room, yelling at someone, and Antsiyanah had never heard him so angry. "Find her or there will be consequences. I swear if anything happens to her-" he stopped as he saw her. "Never mind, Enif found her," he cut the phone and Antsiyanah ran right into his arms.

"I'll come back in a couple of hours to take her for interrogation," Enif said and left the house. Antsiyanah broke down in Clifford's arms and he asked softly,

"What happened? Who took you?"

7

Insensitive

"Alejandro!" Antsiyanah replied, pulling back.

"What-? Why did he take you?"

"He put the Purple Diamond of Mr Francis in my throat, he stole from you."

"It doesn't matter. I don't care about that stupid diamond as long as you are okay. Are you okay?" Antsiyanah shook her head in response, and more tears spilled out of her eyes. She noticed Clifford was crying too. "What else did he do, Antsiyanah?"

"He took Amara, Cliff. He took her away."

"He-what? He took Amara away? But he loved you, and Amara's his daughter, how can he do this to her, take her away from her mother?"

"He spied on us last night. He heard you call me 'An', and he knows you know who I am, and that you've met Amara. He was angry when he found out, and I think he did this because he was mad he didn't get to spend with Amara unlike you. It's all my fault!"

"It's not your fault, Antsiyanah."

"It is. I was insensitive. He went away for me and Amara, he distanced himself from us, for us, and he was in as much pain as I was in, if not more. And I moved on, while he still suffered, and now he hopes for us to get back together, but it's not that simple anymore. I-I just can't go away with him, and a part of me is actually happy that Amara's at least with one of her parents, but another part of me wants to get her back and just make she's okay. It's not that I don't trust him it's just, he's not in his right mind right now. He didn't even notice Amara was bleeding because of him, and as much as I want them two to get close, I just can't help but worry. He could've just asked me; I wouldn't have denied it. But now Amara is scared, and I just-" she couldn't go any further without breaking down.

"How about you go have a nice warm bath which I make you your favourite sundae? Freshen up, Lyric, it will help you get better."

After taking a long bath and dressing into some comfortable clothes, Antsiyanah came out to find Clifford garnishing a sundae.

Clifford was very rich, he could easily ask the cook to make one, or the housekeeping to get one from outside, but he knew she liked the one he made, so he made it for her. That was the thing about Clifford, he was very caring and down to earth. She watched him cook, leaning on the doorframe of the kitchen. He noticed her and smiled warmly at her,

"Get to the table, I'll bring this there."

"No need, I'll just have it here." He raised his eyebrows and Antsiyanah sat on the kitchen counter. She ate the sundae as Clifford watched her. She offered him some which he politely rejected. He looked at her sadly, which she assumed was because she was upset. But something felt off about him. She got off the counter and asked him, "What's wrong, Cliff."

He shook his head, but she knew something was wrong; that there was something he wasn't telling her. She looked at him intently, waiting for him to explain, but he just said, "It's nothing, Lyric."

She took a step closer to him, but her feet felt wobbly, and her head was fuzzy. She realized what he had done. Clifford caught her as she stumbled. "Why?" she managed, barely able to keep herself conscious.

"I am so sorry, Antsiyanah, I am!" he apologized and she was swallowed by the darkness.

When she woke up, she was in an O.I.W interrogation room, tied to a metal chair that was joined to the floor. There was a bright lamp above her, and she knew she wasn't taken to a mere civilized interrogation room like Bellora was. She was in *the* interrogation room. She mentally swore and tried to pretend to be unconscious to save herself but it went noticed.

"We know you're up, so no need to act like you're not." She felt someone slap her cheek, and she looked up to find herself face to face with Carol. "Good girl. Now tell us, who are you?"

"Lyric Bouvier!" Another slap. "I am Lyric Bouvier, who else would I be?"

"I don't know, a spy pretending to be Lyric Bouvier?"

"I am Lyric, I swear!" This time, she got a punch. She tasted blood inside her mouth.

"You're a liar. We showed Lyric's father your picture, and he said it wasn't her. *You* aren't Lyric, and we know it, so don't lie." She coughed the blood out of her mouth. Antsiyanah didn't say anything, Carol punched her again. "I thought you were my friend, but you are a traitor, just like Bellora!"

These people are seriously stupid. Antsiyanah thought, grinning.

"Why are you grinning? Are you enjoying this?"

"Go ahead Carol beat your best friend to a pulp. No hard feelings, right?" Carol hesitated before replying.

"We are not friends!" she punched her in the stomach.

"Carol, I am Lyric. I am not someone else, believe me!"

"Believe you? How-" she was interrupted when by a man who walked into the room.

"She's manipulating you, get out, I'll handle this!" he ordered, and Carol quietly left. "Now, only speak when you are ready to tell us who you are. And if you talk one word of nonsense, I'll rip that perky little tongue of yours, is that understood?" Antsiyanah nodded, trying to look helpless.

"Please...I am Lyric." He punched her, again and again, but she didn't say anything else. She kept on repeating that she was Lyric. She had dealt with pain before and knew she would last for a while, at least until someone got her out of that mess.

She knew who that someone was going to be. She knew Alejandro was going to come to save her, and there was nothing she could do tied to the chair. She ignored the pain, and let the agent, whoever he was, beat her. When he realized punches weren't going to make her crack, he resolved to knives. She didn't even know if he had permission to do that, but the fact that no one was stopping him made her remember that it was a secret agency, and everything was allowed there.

8

Abraham

She wanted to lose her consciousness, but the man was smart, he didn't hit her on her head, knowing she would lose consciousness and would get some peace, and he avoided major arteries, to not let her lose consciousness because of loss of blood.

A part of her was worried she would break and tell them who she was in reality, but she tried her best to hold herself together. If they found out who she was, they would find out about everything, Alejandro, Amara, Adelmo and all their work will go to waste. And it won't be long before they would figure out that she was Mrs Anonymous. So, for her, and everybody else's sake she kept it together, and tolerated all the pain that came towards her.

The man grew impatient with her tolerance. He switched methods, but Antsiyanah remained silent, knowing the consequences of breaking it.

The man left the room, angrily slamming the door shut behind him, and Antsiyanah sighed in relief. Her happiness was short-lived as another person entered the room, and his ID read Abraham.

"Heard you weren't breaking. Tell me, what is your name?"

"Lyric Bouvier."

"Okay, Lyric, the thing is, we know you're not Lyric Bouvier. Now, if you don't tell us your name, we'll have to kill you." Being good at acting, Antsiyanah broke into fake tears.

"I don't care. My husband sold me out, my family doesn't remember me…I have no one!" Abraham crouched in front of her and caressed her cheek.

"So be it. I'll get the executioner ready."

"Thank you…" Antsiyanah feigned sobbing and the Abraham left the room, obviously shocked. Antsiyanah wanted to smile slyly but knew she was being watched. They didn't even know how to make her say one single word.

Abraham got in again and yelled infuriated, "Okay, I am done being nice!" he took out a glowing iron rod. He touched it to her cheeks and she yelped in pain.

"Abraham," A calm voice called and a man got inside. He was neatly dressed and had a file in his hand. "What do you think you're doing?"

"Getting the truth out of this liar!" Abraham dragged the rod down to her neck.

"Hands off her. She's not lying!" Abraham pulled back the rod and turned to him.

"What are you talking about?"

"She's having a psychological problem. She thinks she's Lyric Bouvier, it's what she believes. Her name's Antsiyanah da Silva, and we have orders to let her go back to her husband!"

Abraham smacked her with the rod one last time before letting the man uncuff her. She knew him, he was Leonard, an E.Y.E official of high rank. He escorted her outside and handed her to Enif.

"I told you not to act before we were sure. What have you done to her!"

"I am okay, Enif," Antsiyanah said. Enif looked concerned, and so did Leah, who was standing beside him. She helped Antsiyanah get in a car and drove her back to Clifford's place.

"How are you, Lyric?"

"How am I? Leah, my husband betrayed me! He handed me over to them without even consulting me once. I am far from fine!"

"It was very stupid of him! You want me to take you back to my place?"

"I want to see him once before the E.Y.E officials take me back." Leah nodded and walked her to Clifford, who was waiting for them in the living room. As soon as they got inside, Clifford got up to them.

"I'll let you two talk it out," Saying that, Leah left. Antsiyanah didn't look at Cliff. So he put his hand under her chin and changed her face's position to meet his eyes.

"What have they done to you?" Tears left his eyes, but Lyric neglected them.

"You sold me out!" she cried, frustrated.

'I am sorry, Lyric! They told me you were someone pretending to be Lyric-"

"I am Antsiyanah, pretending to be Lyric. We've talked about this, Clifford. I am so disappointed!"

"I was being an idiot, okay? I am the biggest idiot in the whole world, please, forgive me, Antsiyanah!" she was still mad at him; he was definitely not forgiven. She was about to reply, when the door opened behind them, revealing a very angry Alejandro.

"Alex!" Antsiyanah whispered, as he put his arms around her.

"Are you okay?" Antsiyanah nodded. "Don't worry, I'll kill every last one of them! Why are you standing? You should be resting!" Before Antsiyanah could argue, he turned to Clifford and asked him, "Where's her bedroom?"

Clifford carefully analysed him. He had figured out who he was, and he seemed upset. "Third bedroom right around the corner." He didn't even follow them. Alejandro led her to her bedroom and had her change her clothes while he went to ask Clifford for a first aid kit.

Antsiyanah felt lucky for having two people care for her so deeply. Alejandro ran his fingers on the cuts on her arms and pulled out some antiseptics and bandages. "Alex, no!" she complained as he began to rub it over her cuts. "It hurt!"

"I am sorry. Do you know where the painkillers are? I can get some for you!"

"They are in my drawer!" Antsiyanah had a habit of keeping painkillers in her bedside drawer as a precaution. He gave some to her and she took it and started feeling better. Alex continued bandaging her carefully. Clifford knocked before getting in and sitting beside her. She didn't look at him, because she was mad at him, and she didn't look at Alejandro either, because of the guilt chewing her from the inside.

"Cliff, man, can you get her neck and face?" Alejandro asked Cliff, handing him the first-aid kit. Antsiyanah looked at Alejandro, surprised by what he had just said. Even Clifford was shocked about it but didn't complain as Alejandro handed him the first-aid kit. He added on to her surprise, by leaving the room to give them some space.

"He seems like a nice guy!" Clifford commented putting a bandage on her cheek. "I am sorry I don't know this well!"

9
Rational

"He's nice…I can ask him to go if you want him to!"

"He makes you happy, I can see that, Antsiyanah."

"He makes you uncomfortable, I can see that, Clifford."

"Anything for you. Besides, you are mad at me right now, you could use someone to make you happy."

"You make me happy, I am mad at him too."

"Don't be. He just wanted some time with his daughter, and I don't blame for that, he must've missed her."

"Why are you taking his side?"

"Because I know how much it hurts to be mad at two people close to you!"

"Instead of speaking in your defence, you're speaking in his?"

"I know what I did was wrong, An. I know it was very wrong and there could be no defence for that. But he wasn't all wrong."

"Why are you so nice, Cliff? Why aren't you being possessive or anything? He's my ex-husband for god's sake, I loved him. You should be jealous or something, why are you handling this situation so calmly and rationally?"

"Should I go challenge him to a duel or something?" he asked jokingly.

"I wouldn't advise that, no offence to your fighting skills, but he's highly trained and experienced."

"Right. Well, you know An, it's okay if you feel something for him, I don't mind. I mean it bugs me, but he makes you happy, and I know how relieved you were to see him, it was as if all your pain was gone. An, it's okay to love someone, we can't control our feelings." He nursed her, and after he put on the last bandage, he pulled her out with him to Alejandro. "Talk it out!" he whispered in her ears, making sure only she could hear.

"Feeling better?" Alejandro asked her.

"Sort of."

"I am sorry about earlier. I shouldn't have done that, any of it. And I shouldn't have taken Amara, and I shouldn't have hurt her. And when I found out I had, I hated myself, and I didn't know what to do and-"

"Alejandro, it's okay!" she covered her mouth as soon as she said those words. She realized she had spoken in her original French accent. Her voice seemed foreign to her, she hadn't spoken like that in ages.

"It's okay, Antsiyanah!" he replied in the same accent, and for a moment everything seemed normal. "I'll bring Amara back to you, she's scared out of her mind!"

"She can handle it. It's good for her to have you around. No one can protect her like you can. Just remember she's very sensitive!"

"You sure about this?"

She nodded. "Just tell me where you two are so I can visit sometimes,"

"I'll go back to her now. I'll text you the address. Also, Cliff," he turned to Cliff who was behind Antsiyanah. "You might want to go look for more guards, I sort of killed yours!" he informed nonchalantly before leaving.

"He-what?" Clifford turned to Antsiyanah in confusion. "He was joking, right?"

"I don't think so!" Antsiyanah replied awkwardly.

"You gotta be kidding me!"

"I am sorry, he must've been apprehensive and impatient. I'll help you cover it up."

"Why are you speaking like it's not a big deal and like it's very normal?"

"I have been keeping something from you and you're probably going to hate me for that, but please don't judge me harshly!"

"You've done this before, haven't you? Covering up his murders?"

"I have covered up some of mine too!" Clifford backed away, Antsiyanah didn't know out of fear or resentment. "Listen, please don't freak."

"You're a murderer?"

"I am a serial killer, world-class thief, imposter, spy, and also in love with you. I can explain, all of it."

"I think I understand it all. You're Mrs Anonymous, aren't you?"

"And you are very clever, aren't you? Yes, I am Mrs Anonymous, and Alejandro is Mr Anonymous. I am also Antsiyanah, I didn't lie to you about it. I have killed dozens while working for E.Y.E, they gave me the name Mrs Anonymous and made me kill the bad people in the guise of good people. They couldn't openly do it, since you know, political reasons. So, yes, Cliff, I am a serial killer. I stole those jewels, to make it look like I had a motive and also for E.Y.E. I was eighteen, I used to be a popular thief in my city; I used to do it for fun with Alex. Then they found us and gave us a choice. Die or join E.Y.E. It was not like we had much of a choice. So, we gave in. Honestly, except the killing part, it was nice, really nice."

"Stealing was nice?"

"You think I am the bad guy? Well, Clifford, all those I stole from were the bad guys too. Even your pathetic little Lyric Bouvier! She was bad too, just as bad as anyone else, but no one sees that. You think I am bad, but you don't know a lot, Clifford."

"Then tell me, Antsiyanah. Tell me what I don't know and give me one reason to let it all slide!"

"I am not going to make any excuse or lie and say I was forced, because I wasn't. I was a different person back then."

"Obviously. This person can't even kill a fly, let alone murder a living breathing human being."

"It was thrilling at first. Then it was just tedious. It was nice and fun, showing all the rich people how stupid their security was. I mean, who puts cameras everywhere but on the jewel? Apparently, all the rich people do! I didn't use to enjoy the killings, but it was me or them. I am not as sympathetic, and empathetic and giving and kind as you are."

"Are you kidding me? I have seen you lose sleep to help those people. Was there a selfish reason behind becoming Lyric Bouvier?"

"She had the life I had always wanted, and I loved my life but then Alex died, and I was mad. So, I took her life, decided to come here and make you fall for me because I knew you and Lyric were pretty close, so I wanted to get a stable good life and you turned out to be pretty good. So, yes, it was selfish, cause that's all I am, 'selfish'. I am going to be honest here, and admit that I was only here for selfish reasons!"

"Then why are you here now?"

10
Secrets

"I-I don't know, okay? I don't know anything about it. I just couldn't leave after Alex revealed himself. I wanted to, but at the same time I didn't want to."

"Why?"

"Why are you pushing it? I told you I don't know! You made me cheerful and I guess that's it."

"It's not selfish if you want to be with someone you like. If that was it then everyone would be selfish, An."

"Do you hate me?"

"You're not that person anymore."

"How are you taking this so lightly? You should be mad and you should be yelling and kicking me out. How do you take everything so easily?"

"I am mad and upset. But I can't just yell at you. If you are working with E.Y.E then telling me all this could be a threat for you, and you're still telling me so, I am just glad."

"I am sorry I kept it a secret for so long!"

"I am sorry I sold you out!"

"I'll forgive you if you forgive me!"

"There's nothing for me to forgive, but if that means you will be, then, it's okay. I forgive you!"

"Thank you. I forgive you too. Just talk to me next time!"
"Will do. And no more secrets!" Antsiyanah nodded.

ᗡᗡᗡ

Alejandro went back home to his daughter. Just so she wouldn't try to do something, he had locked her in her room and had shut her window, hoping she wouldn't know how to get out. But it was his daughter, so of course, she knew how to get out.

The door to her room was closed when he got back, just like he had left it. Just to be sure she was inside, he opened it. He wasn't surprised that the room was empty. He knew exactly what she doing. She was trying to get him to peep outside the window so that she could sneak outside the room.

"Where are you? Under the bed?" He concentrated, to hear the slightest of sound. He opened the wardrobe to find himself face to face with Amara, who launched herself at him the second he opened it. He was ready for it, and quickly pinned her arms behind her back. She started kicking him but her kicks were light and they didn't hurt him the slightest bit. "Seriously, Amara, stop, I am not going to kill you." She stopped at that. "I just want to talk!"

She looked at him and then loosened up. "I feel like I know you. Do I?"

"Yes, you know me. We had met when you were very young!"

"Where's my mommy?"

"I got you blueberry muffins. Heard you liked them!" He changed the topic and her eyes lightened up. He had asked Adelmo about what food she liked.

"Thank you!" She replied but did not eat one.

"I haven't poisoned them or anything," He explained. She looked at him with doubt but then ate a muffin. "Have you ever been around Paris?"

She shook her head. "I don't go out a lot."

"Well, there's a lot you have to see then. I brought your clothes from Adelmo. Do you want to have dinner here or outside?"

"Outside would be nice." He put her to sleep after she ate dinner. Adelmo had given him her doll, one she talked to before falling asleep, which he gave her.

She instantly fell asleep and he slept on the chair in her room, afraid to leave her alone. The next day, Alejandro took Amara on a tour of Paris. He was very careful to avoid cameras and to not stay in one place for too long. Amara wasn't highly comfortable around him yet, but when he took her to the mall to a toy store, she started enjoying herself. He bought her three bags full of toys; barbies, cars, dollhouse, kitchen set, and more. He bought everything she looked at, and even the employees were shocked to see him buy so much. He took her back home where together they arranged the dollhouse in another room, along with the other toys.

It wasn't as hard as he thought it would be. Amara wasn't shy, she was very open which made it very easy for him. The best thing about all of it was that Amara wasn't scared of him. He tried to keep his tone soft, and his words kind, which wasn't very difficult seeing Amara was the exact opposite of mischievous.

He brought her snacks and just as he was about to serve them to her, he heard noises. She heard them too and whipped her head to look at him, alarmed.

"I am going to go down and check on them Amara, and you-"

"Stay here, don't move, and make no noise. Hold your gun tight and shoot if anyone but you comes. There's just one problem with that, I don't have my gun, can you give me yours?" he looked at her in awe, he didn't know she knew how to shoot.

"It won't come to that, I'll take care of everything!" But still, for her safety, he handed her one of his guns. The lightest, smallest and easiest to handle. She nodded confidently and hid in a corner beside a cupboard. Amara seemed to be trained well because she knew just what to do.

He walked down the stairs, outside his front door to the yard where Antsiyanah was standing right outside her car.

"Wasn't expecting you so soon,"

"Thought I should check-in. How are you two doing?"

"Pretty great. How have you been? Physically and mentally?"

"I told Cliff I am Mrs Anonymous!"

"How did he take it?"

"I am not sure, pretty maturely I think."

"That's good, right?"

"I am not sure about that either!" she mumbled, looking at her feet. "Can I see Amara?" He looked at her, confused. He wasn't sure why she was asking him for permission. He nodded quietly and led her inside. Antsiyanah looked moody, so he avoided conversation and led her straight to Amara. "Amara..." she called and Amara quickly jumped out of her hiding spot into Antsiyanah's arms and instantly starts crying.

"I've missed you. Are you here to take me back home?"

"I have good news for you, honey." Without looking at him, she reached out a hand towards him, which he took and walked closer to both her and Amara. "You are going to live with your dad from now on! Isn't that exciting?"

11
Exceptional

Alejandro looked at her, shocked, and just as he was about to react to that, Amara did, "My dad? I thought-"

"This is Alejandro," Antsiyanah interrupted. "And he is your father, darling." Amara didn't seem to be taken aback by this, she looked as if she was expecting this. "Now, how about you play here for a bit while I and your dad talk for a bit?" Amara nodded and went off to play with her new toys while Antsiyanah pulled Alejandro out of the room.

"Are you sure about this? You taught her how to use a gun?"

"She's in the E.Y.E training!"

"Are you kidding me?"

"I don't want her to be like us, I want her to be one of the 'good guys' and an exceptional one while she's at it!"

"What about what she wants?"

"She's too young to decide."

"She might not like this decision when she grows up!"

"I know that. But if I don't train her to be exceptional, she might not like that either. How do I know what she is going to like in the future? How do I know what she would want to be when she grows up? Do you know how confusing it is?" He didn't argue and Antsiyanah left after having a discussion about Leighton.

ᑭᑭᑭ

For once, Antsiyanah was sure that she had done something right. She knew Amara had the right to spend time with her father, and she knew Amara would need someone who was her own, to take care of her, after she was gone.

She pushed her thoughts aside and focused on the problem on their hand. She drove to Leighton's house. It was Leighton's day off, and Antsiyanah was temporarily suspended from E.Y.E due to everyone thinking she had a mental disorder.

Leighton was arrogantly friendly. She was over-confident but tried her best to be humble. Leighton had honey-blonde hair that came to her shoulder. She was great at strategizing and combat-fighting. She was the kind of person who could possibly be Mrs Anonymous.

So, Antsiyanah rod right into her house with the excuse of having a 'tea' with her. Leighton gracefully invited her into the house, and Antsiyanah carefully checked that no one was around. Antsiyanah quietly plopped down on the couch which Leighton brought her tea.

"How have you been? Enif told me about your...illness."

"I am great, still figuring things out, I mean I just realized people can be so dumb."

"What do you mean?"

"Sit!" Antsiyanah ordered, and Leighton frowned.

"Just cause you are sick does not mean you can go around bossing people!"

"I tried!" Antsiyanah sighed to herself and took out her gun and pointed it at Leighton. "Sit, or I will kill you!"

"Lyric, what are you-"

"How long is it going to take you to figure out that I am not Lyric!"

"Who are you then?"

"Sit and we'll talk!" Leighton obeyed. She sat back down and Antsiyanah put her gun away, she knew she didn't need it. "Good girl. So, Leighton, I am the famous Mrs Anonymous. And now, you are going to go to a high-ranking E.Y.E official, and you are going to tell him that you are Mrs Anonymous."

"But it's you!"

"I know, I usually don't let people take credit for what I did, but hey, if it helps, the official is going to know you're not Mrs Anonymous, and that I am! The senior officers know."

"What do you mean?"

"I am an E.Y.E Agent, name: Antsiyanah da Silva, Code name: Mrs Anonymous!"

Leighton's eyes widened in shock and Antsiyanah rolled hers. "That's sick! E.Y.E ordered the kill of all those innocents?"

"They weren't innocents, silly. I'll tell you everything...maybe. For now, do as I said."

"Why?"

"Huh? That's a great question, I never thought about it. Your son's at his kindergarten, right? Right beside the old cemetery. And your husband's...right, with god."

"Wh-what are you talking about?"

"Just kidding. But he will be with the god if you don't do as I just said!" Leighton made a grab for her gun but Antsiyanah shot her in the arm before she could even reach it. "You had that coming! Now, do we have a deal?"

"No! No way. You shot me! We are friends!"

Antsiyanah exhaled. She was getting tired. Her real sickness wasn't a mental disorder, if possible, it was something *way* worse. She started feeling dizzy but managed to keep herself awake. She got up, still pointing her gun at Leighton and said, "Do as I said. I don't want to threaten your child, Leighton. Just do I say!" she ran outside the house to her car and drove away after taking her medicines.

The next day, Enif called her, informing her that Leighton had admitted that she was Mrs Anonymous, so they had set Bellora somewhat free. He had also told her that Leighton had told him that Mr Anonymous was dead and that was why she was turning herself in; out of guilt.

Antsiyanah controlled her smirk. Her plan had gone just as she wanted it to go. The lower E.Y.E officials would be satisfied by it and didn't have the power to do or question anything unless the higher officials permitted it and the higher officials were the ones who made her Mrs Anonymous, so, she knew she and Alejandro were in clear.

She knew how to keep everyone out of danger and to keep their names clean. Everyone thinking she was psycho was *way* better than everyone finding out she was Mrs Anonymous.

12

Chameleon

It had been a few days since Leighton had turned herself in. Everything had been quiet. She used to stay at home and had a therapist see her every now and then. The therapist was actually an E.Y.E agent, Camaleonte, a very high profiled officer. She was known to be the master of disguise, and very few high ranking officials in the E.Y.E knew about her missions and work. Camaleonte knew all about Antsiyanah's identity, so, she just used to pretend to be asking about her life because of all the cameras present in the therapy room.

The lower officials monitored them, but they didn't see through the act. She would go to therapy thrice a week and spend the rest of her time at home. She couldn't go see Amara or Alejandro; she couldn't risk anyone following her. Normally, she would be going out of her mind if she didn't see Amara at least once every two days, but surprisingly, she was less worried since Amara was with Alejandro. But that didn't mean she didn't mean her. She was her daughter, and she missed her more than anyone or anything.

Cliff noticed her sorrow and tried soothing her, but she had kept her distance from him. Everything would've been so much easier if she didn't *love* him. If he wasn't so good, so caring, so understanding. She was grateful for having him around; she knew she couldn't have taken the loss of Alejandro without him. He helped her cope, and he was okay with all her pretences, all her secrets, all her lies. Sure, he was hurt she hadn't told him earlier but had never argued much. Sometimes, it felt too good to be true.

Lately, he had been home with her as much as he could. He had a lot of work, but he was kind enough to skip a lot of it just to spend time with her. She appreciated it but felt immense guilt for holding him back.

Out of blue, one day, before going to bed, Cliff presented her with a set of platinum earrings that were beautifully embedded with Alexandrites and diamonds. They were long and had thin wired designs.

"This is so not fair! I didn't get you anything, I never get you anything!" she moaned complainingly.

"You know I really don't mind, right?" he smiled at her after putting away the earrings. "I wanted to ask you something. It might seem very nosey, and um...too much. But...I don't know where to start. How's Amara?"

"She's doing great...I believe. I haven't met her in a while. I am guessing you have something to say about Amara."

"I know how much being away from her hurts you, and I just wanted to offer you something. We can adopt her. I mean you're her mother, but um...no one but me knows that and so we can..." his voice trailed off, leaving Antisiyanah's eyes wide.

"You would do that for me?" Antsiyanah asked, with her eyes wide, pooling with tears.

"I know how much she means to you, An. I know how much joy that will bring you!"

She threw her arms around him, as tears of joy trailed down her eyes. "Thanks, Cliff. But I don't think Alejandro would like it. It will immensely hurt him, and I don't want to do that!"

"Talk to him once, okay? I called him here, he should be here in a while. I want you to consider it. Amara's just like my daughter, and I am sure even she wants to spend her childhood with her mother living in a proper home."

She didn't believe her ears. She always knew Clifford was kind, but she never thought he would care so much for her. Alejandro arrived in a few minutes, and he was more than shocked to find Antsiyanah in tears.

"An, you okay?"

"There's something I need to ask you, but you have to promise not to kill me!" he smiled at that.

"I won't kill you, I promise. What is it?"

"Cliff asked if we can adopt Amara!"

"You are her mother!"

"Yes, but no one knows that. So, he was wondering if we can move her with us, legally making it seem like we adopted her from an orphanage."

"So, she calls him dad?"

"She can call him Cliff! I just had to ask you, if you have a problem with it, then we can choose not to do it!"

"Antsiyanah, I am going to do something that's going to hurt you, but for once, I am going to let get impulse best of me!" Before she could register what he said, he took out a syringe and injected her with an instant paralyze causing drug. He tied her up with a pillar and went inside the house. All she heard was noises of struggle and he came back outside with a knife pressed against Clifford's throat. A tear escaped her eye. She knew what he was going to do. She tried to move but miserably failed. It was a temporary drug, which wore off in a couple of minutes, enough time for him to tie Clifford up too.

"A..." Antsiyanah managed. "Please...."

"I am sorry, An. But I just can't take it anymore!" Clifford struggled to break free as Alejandro brought a gun towards his head.

"Please, A, please don't do this..." she begged, hoping for him to stop, but he didn't. All she heard was a loud *bang*, and Clifford's blood sprawled across her face. "No!" she screamed in agony and Alejandro put his gun back in, with no sign of remorse on his face. "What did you do!" she screamed. "How could you?" he didn't reply, and she finally cut her ropes off using a cutter from a pocket. If only she had done it earlier...

"I wanted to let her be with her father, but I didn't want to leave her with you, you psychopath! *You* had brought it all upon yourself! How could you do this? He mattered to me, to Amara; yes, she and he were hell close. They went boating together, and to picnics. Good luck explaining to your daughter what happened to her third favourite person in the world. And for your information, you don't make the top ten. You know, you are not even going to chance to explain yourself. Amara and I, are done with you!"

"Amara is with me, An. You are the one who's going to be alone."

13

Time's Up

Antsiyanah scoffed in response. "I was afraid you would run away with Amara at the slighted mention of this proposal; so, I asked Adelmo to take her back when you were here! Though I never thought you would stoop this low, but you are going to deserve this!"

"You wouldn't dare, An."

"I thought the same thing. Guess we both just keep surprising each other! Go to hell, A. And before you even try to think of killing me, know that Amara will never be in your reach and you will lose your chance on making up to us!" It gave him hope that there was the slightest chance that he could clean this mess, and killing her had never crossed his mind. "Leave me be, A. I don't want to see you right now!" he didn't argue and left, almost feeling no guilt. But something felt heavy in his chest. He knew he shouldn't have done it; but he pushed the thought aside, convincing himself that it was necessary.

He could hear her loud sobs across the house, and it brought him pain. He drove his car, as fast as he could, back to his place, praying to god to keep his Amara there, but found the house empty. He found a piece of paper on his dining table. A small letter was written in pink crayon in messy cursive,

Dearest Daddy!

Adelmo came to get me back to mommy. He told me she misses me. I will be back soon, so please don't clear up my barbie-set. I promise we'll play with my tea-set when I get back.

Love,

Amara

He held it close in his arms, knowing that it might be the last letter his daughter would ever write to him. He knew that she would hate him once she figured out that he had killed Clifford.

He knew he would never be able to get used to the silence now. He knew he would miss the made-up stories his daughter made with her dolls, the clanking of her glass tea-set, the zooming of the toy cars; and the crayon paintings on his walls would always remind him of his mistake.

His phone rang and the caller id read, 'Adelmo'. He didn't pick up the call, knowing the reason behind it. He didn't want Adelmo to yell at him about killing Clifford.

He received a text within seconds of him cutting the phone. It read,

E.Y.E broke its deal. They have captured Antsiyanah. Amara's safe with me. RUN!

He grabbed his emergency pack and jumped inside his car and drove as fast as he could. He didn't take a single breath of peace until he was a safe distance from his house and then called Adelmo.

"Where have they taken Antsiyanah?"

"To their base."

"I'll get there. You get Amara out of Europe, now! Get her somewhere out of E.Y.E's reach. I'll call you later, I got a base to destroy."

***

Antsiyanah tugged at the cuffs binding her to the chair. She was surrounded by her colleagues; Enif, Leighton, Carol, Bellora and others. They were giving her angry glares.

"You are to be handed over to the government and you will get at least a death sentence." Enif sighed, shaking his head.

"Not interested, sorry," Antsiyanah replied.

"You pretended to be Lyric Bouvier and then pretended to have a psychological disorder? How low are you going to stoop?"

"You think I stooped low? The 'psychological disorder' was not my idea. It was E.Y.E's."

"What do you mean?"

"I am E.Y.E.'s creation. I was trained by E.Y.E to become Mrs Anonymous. Everything I did, was on E.Y.E's command. I am not the only villain in this story!"

"What are you talking about?" Bellora asked.

"E.Y.E made me who I am. I was just a PhD doctor, then E.Y.E chose to make me more!"

"She's lying!" Carol accused, stomping her foot.

"No, she's not. E.Y.E is a villain too!" Leighton stated, crouching in front of Antsiyanah. "Where are you going with this?"

Antsiyanah smiled deviously before replying, "I'll make you all a deal. I'll help you clean E.Y.E and you all let me go free!"

"As if!"

"Hear me out. I will give you the names of all the corrupted officers, you can get rid of them-"

"As in kill them?"

"Hand them to the government or whatever you please. I will even help you. This is your one chance."

"One chance? You are the one tied up. You should be seriously begging!" Antsiyanah shook her head in disbelief. She was shocked at how stupid everyone was. Any sane person would know that she would easily break free. "Why did you kill Clifford?"

Rage flashed in Antsiyanah's eyes. Her hands balled into fists and her nails dug into her skin, drawing blood. "I did not kill him!" she snarled through her clenched teeth.

"Who did it?" Carol questioned.

"Alejandro did. He killed Cliff!"

"Are you kidding me? Why did he do that?"

"Personal issues!"

"So your one lover killed another one? What a tragic love story!"

"Honey, tragedy is going to happen to you if you don't shut up."

"You're the one in handcuffs; you should not threaten your captures!" She did not like being reminded of Clifford. He had died because of her, and not once had he blamed her. He never even got mad at her. He was always so caring and understanding; sometimes Antsiyanah got scared that she would never be able to repay his kindness.

Thinking about him hurt now. She knew she would never see him again. Even if she died, she would go to hell; and someone as sympathetic as Cliff would be in no place but heaven. A tear escaped the cage of her lashes; which as much as she hoped, did not go unnoticed.

"Is the big bad Mrs Anonymous crying?"

"Leave her be, Carol!" Enif intervened. "What's wrong, Lyric?"

"Okay, we're done talking," Antsiyanah replied abruptly. "Now, time's running. Do we have a deal or not?"

"You're heartless!" A loud bang erupted a little away from them and a smile crept up on Antsiyanah's face.

"*Beep!* Time's up."

14

Parting Ways

Alejandro watched as the exit of the building went down in flames. He knew exactly where she was being held captive. He could hear the screams coming from inside the building; which all roared 'victory'. People were running out of the building, and some were calming the fire. The doctors were brought to safety by the fighters, and Alejandro walked into the building through the entrance; taking advantage of the commotion. People were so caught up evacuating the space, they did not notice him. They were protecting themselves from fire; while they should've been protecting themselves from *him.*

Another bomb went down on the building's east side. Alejandro pulled out his revolver and shot an agent evacuating some new recruits. E.Y.E was going to pay for betraying both of them. Another bomb went off on the west side. All the exists were blocked by fire and blood was sprawled everywhere.

Alejandro smoothly made his way through all the chaos to where Antsiyanah was being held. He killed anyone who crossed his way. He opened the door and found Antsiyanah tied to a chair, barely conscious with blood dripping down her face. She was surrounded by about six to seven people and all of them turned to face the door the second he entered. He was about to shoot them when he heard Antsiayanah groan, "No, A, don't kill them they are my friends!"

"Friends who have you in chains."

"Alejandro, please. They'll help us destroy E.Y.E!"

"We will do no such thing!" Leighton, he assumed, answered. Alex shot her without wasting another moment and Antsiyanah screamed.

"Al, please, stop, please. Stop killing everyone!" A part of him wanted to show her that those people weren't her friends, but even though he was blinded by rage, he managed to stop himself and instead, simply and cautiously, broke her bonds. Stumbling, she got up. He put an arm around her waist to stable her. She hugged him and slowly whispered in his ear. "Kill them all." He could feel her reach for his gun in his pocket and she turned around, and both of them, at the same time shot them all dead. All but Enif. "Sorry Enif, but this all had to happen."

Alejandro took her out from the only exit, not on fire. He drove her away, and as if on cue, the last bomb went off, and he caught one last glance of the building turning to ash.

Antsiyanah looked out of the window, and he softly asked her, "How are you, An?"

"I am good."

"I am sorry." He said after a long peaceful silence. I am so sorry for killing Clifford, I really didn't mean to; I swear I didn't mean to. I was impulsive and stupid, please forgive me." he turned to her, hoping to hear an answer, but found her asleep. He continued driving them to a safe house that E.Y.E did not know of and woke her up when they got there.

She was still sleepy, so he saw her composure drop, and noticed her limp. "An, everything okay?"

"Mm-hmm." She replied but almost tripped.

"Yeah, right!" he commented sarcastically and helped her get inside the house. He walked her to the couch and had her seated there while he checked her injuries.

"Thanks, Alejandro." She again fell asleep on the couch and he moved her in her room on her bed after he tended to her wounds.

He knew something was wrong with her; he just couldn't find out what. She had turned weaker and he had kept an eye on her for a while and he had noticed she was getting more sleep than usual. He remembered the time she had started coughing violently when he had kidnapped her. He would've believed it was because of the stone he had put in her throat but he saw Adelmo give her the medicines as if something like that was going to happen.

A part of him believed she would tell him if something was wrong with her health, but another part of him was sure that she wouldn't want to worry him.

The next morning, he woke up to her making breakfast. Despite her injuries, her movements remained undaunted. She served the breakfast on the table, and both of them ate silently.

"I am leaving this evening." She stated, not looking at him in the eye.

"Where are you going?"

"To Amara and Adelmo."

"And I am guessing you are not going to tell me where." She looked away. "An, she's my daughter, I have the right to stay with her!"

"Don't you get it? You killed Cliff! You murdered my husband ruthlessly right in front of my eyes! And he meant a lot to Amara too, A! We can't just pretend to be a merry little family!"

"You don't even want to give it a shot!" Antsiyanah got up.

"I am going, Alejandro, we are done!"

"Go wherever you want Antsiyanah, you will come back. Or I will find you. And then, you will be the one who'll be away from Amara!"

Antsiyanah laughed bitterly. "We'll see, Alejandro, we'll see!"

The Hues Of Samsara

My life was always different, even when I didn't know about it. But it supposedly changed after I had the worst headache of my life. And sometimes I wish the secrets were kept secret; for when revealed, they made everything a thousand times worse.

I exhaled, holding my head. I had the urge to bang my head against the wall, but I knew it would only make the pain worse. I was having crazy dreams, that lead to headache due to my best hobby; overthinking, and I had spent my whole afternoon searching for ways to deal with the headache. One thing about headaches: they are the worst. Had it been a stomachache or some type of body ache, I could just distract myself by watching TV or reading or studying or something. But with headache, it only made things worse; and it invited my worst demon: boredom to pounce at me. The pain was easier to deal with than boredom. Because when I am bored, I think, which causes more headache. I closed my eyes, trying to sleep but an image from my nightmare appeared. A little girl running on the roof of the apartments I lived in, and someone pushing her off, and she falling to death. I had this kind of dream before, when I was five. A baby thrown from the roof of a castle. I had an excellent memory when it came to dreams. Somehow, I remembered every detail; which surprised everyone but me.

I got up. I hated doing nothing. It was a waste of time, which I hated. I sat on my chair near my study table. My diary laid open in front of me. I grabbed a black marker from my pencil stand and started doodling on my arm. I drew two symbols: a crescent shaped moon behind the trapezium of my thumb, and a circle with a half circle and a plus symbol beneath it.

I had no idea where it came from, but I just felt the need to draw it. Over the years, I had learnt many things. Let me reframe it. Over the years, I have learnt everything possible. From drawing to singing to dancing to everything. Even some weird things like fencing and Latin and different symbols from different mythologies and looming.
The symbol felt familiar. I got up and took out another diary from my shelf: the one in which I note all the symbols I learn and their meanings. I flipped pages to the Alchemy section. It was filled with the symbols used by the Alchemists in the ancient times. I turned some pages until I saw the symbol. Beneath the symbol I had written: Pluto. For a careless moment, I thought it was nothing until, it hit me. It wasn't just the symbol of Pluto. It was also the symbol of death. Chills ran down my spine. I tried to convince myself it was a mere coincidence, but I couldn't. Because I knew, it wasn't. The reasons I studied different symbols was because I doodled them around; symbols whose meaning I knew not. And then I searched their meaning on the internet. Then, I started researching different symbols. I often had dreams about different symbols and languages. So, I started learning different languages too. I knew, three Indian, three European and an international language. I know how to write in Morse code and runes. And, I am thirteen. I am captain of two sports teams in my school and the class topper since kindergarten. I am what other mothers call, "Good example!"
I have friends, a lot of them. Best friends too. But I am a girl who loves shadows. That's where I stay. In the shadows. Apart from my achievements, people don't pay me much

attention. Let me correct that sentence; Apart from my achievements, people didn't pay me much attention. But that was until I drew that symbol on my arm. Which changed everything, I stood for. I stood for someone who no one tangled with, because they knew better. I stood for the good quiet girl, no one paid much attention, I stood for revenge, the sweet taste of vengeance. For excellence. Now, I stand for forgiveness, for using silence as a voice not a way to hide in the shadows, for being noticed, for perfection, for precision, and above all, for being a hunter.

This is all present. I'll take you six months into the past. Back to the day, the moment, I drew that symbol; the symbol of the devourer, the end, the inevitable, or so I thought.

The symbol stood out on my pale white arm. And for once, I felt glad that I was having a headache, for I couldn't overthink about the symbol. At least not at that moment. I grabbed my purse and walked outside my room to my grandma's.

"Granny, can I go to the pharmacy? I couldn't find the medicine for my headache. I think I misplaced it somewhere."

"What's that symbol?" she questioned; worry lines deepening on her face.

"I just doodled it by mistake. It's nothing."

"It's not nothing. It's the symbol of death."

"How do you know that?"

"I have studied on that particular subject. But the 'how' is not important. The 'why' is important."

"I told you, I drew it by mistake. It was an involuntary action."

"You should be more careful. Drawing symbols like this: never ends well."

"What do you mean?"

"Go get the medicine you wanted. We'll talk later." I nodded, I knew better than to question her decision. I took the key of our house and closed the door behind me as my grandma settled for her fifteen minutes evening beauty sleep. I walked below the early evening sky, sun blazing in front of my eyes. The pharmacy store was nearby. Right around the corner, as my dad said. I used my purse to block the sunlight and turned around the corner. As usual, a middle age man sat on the counter with a table lamp and few other medical stuff. The shop was covered with green wallpaper and the chemist was reading a newspaper. I had been there before twice, once with my grandma, and once with my brother Reyansh; but I had never noticed anything. At that time, I felt the urge to observe everything. The newspaper was of the previous day, I noted. Then mentally yelled at myself for that. I had bigger problems. Behind me, two men entered the shop. They looked like they were in their twenties and they were whispering something to each other. The chemist heard them and put down his newspaper. "How long have you been here? I am sorry if I didn't notice you."

"It's alright. I just got here."

"So, what do you want?"

"A little help. My head hurts, so I am sure what medicine I should take. I was thinking aspirin, but honestly, I am sure."

"I'll give you something mild." He said smiling. He rummaged around and came back with a box of tablets.

"Thank you." He removed his spectacles, and handed me the medicines. Reading lenses. I noted.

"Sir you want something?" he asked the men behind me. They turned to face him, their face mixed with anger and confusion.

"Excuse me?" one of them asked.

"He's asking if you want any help."

"No, we're fine." The other one replied, his eyebrows raised.

"Um…okay," I paid the chemist who was staring at me, in wonder and confusion.

"What's your name?" the first man asked.

"Grandma says not tell strangers my name."

"But we're not strangers, are we?" his accent turned thick and I realized something. That was the first time we talked in English. We weren't talking in Hindi before. Or Gujarati. We were talking in foreign languages. European. Spanish, French and Latin. In that perfect order.

"Do I know you?" I asked in English, trying to calm myself.

"It's a nice tattoo. I can sense death around you."

"I have to go." I spoke bluntly and ran outside the store. The strangers didn't follow. I unlocked my house as fast as I could and entered. I closed the door behind me. "Grandma! Grandma!" I called. No reply. I rushed to her room. She was sleeping peacefully on her bed. A little too peacefully. Death symbol. Negative thoughts rushed into my brain. I shook her. She didn't move. I pushed my thoughts aside and called her name several times. She didn't answer. I called my father, who was at work.

"Dad, it's nanny. She's not moving."

"Calm down, tell me more precisely, what happened?"

"Nanny was taking her nap and now she's not waking up!"

"Call the ambulance, I'll get there." I took out my nanny's phone and called the ambulance. A lady picked up the phone. I told her it was an emergency and told her my address. She told me the ambulance will arrive within half an hour, so I sat down to wait. By the time the ambulance came, i tried moving my nanny, but she didn't move. I had called my brother Reyansh who arrived just in time for the ambulance to come. They took my nanny's pulse, which I could've checked, but I was too afraid. Afraid to face the reality. My mom had died when I was young, so my nanny took care of me, and now I didn't know if I could handle it if she died too.

TWO
Hunter's Hearing

My brother took my hand to comfort me while they checked her pulse. They told me something I already knew; there was no pulse. No breathing. They checked if she was really dead or just brain dead. But she really was dead. Gone forever. I controlled tears that were threatening to fall off, I didn't wish to cry. I could just think of one thing; if she died because I drew that symbol. It seemed impossible. But the coincidence was too much to take. My brother called my dad and from the expression on his face, I could tell he was barely holding himself together. We called some other relatives of ours. My grandma's sister, was the first to arrive. She was a lot like grandma, the same cheery self, but right now, even she was grim. We did the rituals. My nanny's body was to be burnt the other day, by which all our relatives had arrived. Everyone was crying hysterically. Everyone but me. I managed to stop my tears until they moved the body, when my control over my tears broke, and I wept on my aunt Krishna's shoulder, who held me. Everyone but my maternal aunt Krishna, maternal uncle Kedar, and my aunt Krishna's son, Vihaan, who was my brother Reyansh's age, left. I haven't told you much about my brother. He was every definition of cool. He cared a lot for me, loved me a lot. He wanted to be an interior designer, so, he had a designer's head, so our whole house was designed by him and me.

My cousin, was a typical brother. He wasn't cool, but protective. It was like he was my real brother. He was close my brother's age, around twenty-three. We often went to national parks and science exhibitions together. He was studying medical and he had his exams coming over in a month or so; but still, he had agreed to spend the night with us. That was the thing I liked the most about him, he put family above all. We put up an extra bed for him in me and my brother's room. At around eight, we had dinner, which was cooked by our relatives at their place. They brought it over to our place and we all ate together. It wasn't much. Just normal sabji, roti and rice. During dinner, everyone tried to make small talk, but with a dead body in your house, believe me, it wasn't easy. My aunts looked at me and my brother with pity and my aunt Krishna, even talked to me in private, saying that if I ever needed a mother, she would always be there. My aunt Krishna is nice. Very much like my mother, as people say, but I would never know, since my mom died when I was five.

It was just another normal day, I had woken up in the morning from the night I mentioned before, about a baby thrown from a castle's roof, and I started crying. My dad woke up and soothed me, my mom didn't. She never woke up. In the morning, dad tried waking her up but it was useless. I was too young, so I didn't understand what was happening, my brother Reyansh did. He took me to another room and told me that mom had gone for a long sleep like bears did every winter. And that she would wake up and come back by the end of the winter. But she didn't. I spent my day with my cousin brother, Vihaan, at his place. Everyone acted normal around me, but even the five-year-old me knew everything wasn't normal. Something was wrong, I told my brother Vihaan my nightmare that day. He looked at me worried and told me not to worry. I still remember his eyes widening with apprehensiveness when I asked him if my nightmare had something to do with my mom going into a deep slumber. He didn't reply, he just hugged me and said that everything would be fine. That winter, I stayed with my aunt Krishna and her husband, my uncle Abhra for a while with my brother. Then for a while with my uncle Kedar and his wife Tulsi. They all treated me like their daughter, but I missed my mom. Because mom is mom, she's irreplaceable. My nanny's death was like a replay of my mother's death. I sat with my brothers, Reyansh and Vihaan. We sat in silence for a while before I spoke.

"Something happened today." They both glanced over in concern.

"What happened?" my brother Reyansh asked me worriedly.

"I went to the chemist for a headache medicine-"

"You went alone? I have told you not to go alone outside the house!" brother Reyansh interrupted.

"Let her complete!"

"Thanks brother Vihaan. I met two men, who talked to me in Spanish, French and Latin and I didn't realize that until they talked to me in English. And then they told me they smelled death around me and that we weren't strangers. But I had never seen them before in my life. And then I came home, more like ran home and I found nanny dead. And a little time before I left, I subconsciously drew the symbol of death on my hand. What's happening, brothers?" tears rolled down my cheek and brother Reyansh put an arm around me to sooth me.

"Nothing's happening to you. Just get some sleep. You are

overthinking." I nodded. Brother Reyansh and Vihaan exchanged glances and I could see a silent agreement going on between them. They were hiding something, I knew it, but I was too tired to care. I turned off the lights and pulled up the sheets and went to sleep.

I woke up at around midnight, to the sound of approaching footsteps. I could tell there were two people, and from the sound of the footsteps, they were both adults. I heard the main door of the house close and I could hear both the people enter.

"Today there were two, tomorrow there would be dozens."

"Nani's soul covers her. She is safe."

"For now. We need to call Amara. She is the only person who can protect her!"

"Have you lost your mind? Amara? You know every time Amara gets involved, she dies. He follows her. Wherever Amara goes, he follows. He'll kill her like the last five times."

"Kill who?" I asked standing upright, when the footsteps stopped inside my room. In the faint moonlight, I could see both my brothers Reyansh and Vihaan at my door.

"We were talking about a video game, Sarika. Just go back to sleep." Brother Vihaan told me softly.

"A video game? Since when do you play a video game?" I asked sleepily. "And what were you doing out of the house at this hour of night."

"We went downstairs to feed a dog." Brother Reyansh answered, hesitantly.

"You went downstairs to feed a dog, at three in the morning? At least make some convincible excuse." I yawned and pressed my head back into the pillow. "I am going back to sleep."

They walked out to the veranda and due to my dizziness, I could vaguely hear them speaking to each other.

"Don't call Amara. She's danger. He'll follow her and he'll kill her." He said the other her as if he wasn't talking about Amara.

"Look, she's our only chance. And she would've learnt from her mistakes, right? I mean you think the sixth time she would be a little more careful?"

"There has to be another way. She's safe for now. We still have a couple years-"

"Shush...."

"What?"

"Her hunter skills. She can hear us." Brother Vihaan reduced his voice so much, I could barely make out that line.

"Look, I told my friend to set a trap for the enemy when it enters. Now, let's get back to sleep. We'll play it after they burn nanny's body." Brother Reyansh spoke in normal voice. I was so tired, that I couldn't quite understand what as going on, and before I knew, I was asleep again.

THREE
Control Over Life

Death is inevitable. We have no control over it. But what about our life? How do we control it? Do we control it. How much control do we have over our life? I believe, the answer is zero per cent. We have zero control over life. The more we try to bring it in control, the more it goes out of control. Humans have tried to control nature. But the thing is, life, like nature, doesn't like to be controlled. The more we try to control it the more it goes out of control. What happens when we try to control a tornado? Can we control it? No. Nature is the only thing that can control nature. Just like that, life and nature are the only things that can control life. The life of someone else controls over life, our fate. Some stranger might have made a big change in your life and you might not have known it. Something funny done by someone else, makes us laugh. Makes our life enjoyable. The only we have control over, is our mind and body. How we control our mind against things and how we take care of our body.

Some people want control over everybody's life. Imagine being in control of everyone's lives. Imagine having control over everything. Decisions are hard to make. Imagine being have to make decisions over everybody's lives. And imagine the responsibility coming with it. Imagine the pressure. People losing their money, lives, because of your decisions. It could drive you insane. It could drive anyone insane. Therefore, you have no control over your life, the only thing you have control over, is your own self. Your self-growth, your health, your hobbies. Life goes on. It always will, you can't stop it. You can't control it. What you can do, is keep up with it. Go on with it. The more you try to bring it in control, the more it will go out of control.

So, it is just better if we have control over just two things. Two very important things. Our mind. And our body. And leave the rest to fate and hope for the best.

FOUR
Weighing Losses

Dear diary,

Death. It scares me, for it is quite terrifying. Life is depicted as a journey with a destination. But I don't think life is as simple as that. I believe, life is story, a story with no end. I don't believe death is the end. My culture believes in reincarnation. So, if our soul goes on, how is death an end? Souls are immortal, indestructible and eternal, so how is death an end to something that has no end? I believe death is just a phase in the eternal life of the soul. And I wonder, why we fear death. Why I fear death. I wonder how my mother is. Has she had another reincarnation or is she with the god, I wonder.

I can't take the loss of my grandma. I loved her. She was the closest thing I ever had to a mother. I don't know, why she died. I don't know why god took her away. I tell myself everything happens for a reason, but what could be the reason for her death. And I wonder what my brothers meant when they said that nanny's soul covers me? Was it my fault she died? I drew that symbol and maybe that's what caused her death. Or maybe I am overthinking. But I can't stop thinking. I can't stop blaming myself. Today, they burned her. I stayed back with my aunts while the men in the family went to the cemetery. I cried real bad and caused everyone else to cry more than they already were. They say she's still around me, with me and somehow I can feel her presence. But I don't see her. And I badly want to. She wanted to tell me something, but because of my stupid headache, I will never find out what she wanted me to know.
Sarika

I didn't usually write in a diary; I only wrote when I really needed to talk to someone, and I had no one. My brothers were hiding something from me. They wouldn't seriously be talking about video games when our grandma had died. They faced grief and moreover had decency.

All the men went to the cemetery, while the women stayed back. For a while, everyone stayed quiet. Then they started having small talk. I sat alone in my room and cried to myself. Now and then, someone would come in the room for something and would see me crying and start crying themselves; which made me feel like everyone would've been happier if I hadn't been there. At last, my aunt Krishna entered the room to see me. She was crying and I could here commotion behind her which indicated the men had returned from burning my nanny's body.

"They're back. You shouldn't sit here alone. I'll send Vihaan and Reyansh to keep you company. And talk to them, they're your brothers." I nodded. "And I'll tell them to close the door behind them."

"Whatever you say, aunty." She left and few minutes later, my brothers entered. "She's really gone, isn't she? She never gonna come back." I asked.

"We need to talk." Brother Reyansh said.

"Go ahead."

"Your school starts back tomorrow. You need to go there, you need to get our mind off things. We have told your class teacher what has happened. She has said that the teachers will lay off you for a while. And it's fine if you haven't done your weekend's homework."

"I did it on Friday evening. It was about family background. Nanny helped me with it." Brother Reyansh sighed and sat beside me along with brother Vihaan. He put an arm around me and I started sobbing. He gently patted my back while brother Vihaan poured me a glass of water from the jar of water on my beside table. I took the glass from him and sipped down the whole glass.

"So, who's Amara?"

"Who's who?" Brother Vihaan asked blankly.

"Amara. That girl you were thinking of calling when you went down to feed the dogs at three in the morning."

"Feed dogs-at three? Sarika, are you okay?" Brother Vihaan asked worriedly.

"Really? Now you're gonna pretend that didn't happen?"

"Sarika, you should really rest. You cried yourself to sleep last night; you must've had a dream."

"It wasn't a dream. I asked you who was Amara and you said you were talking about a video game."

"Do you seriously think we would be talking about video games on the night of our grandmother's death?" I shook my head. "See, right there you got your answer!" I was confused. There were chances it could be a dream, but I believed what I say, and I believed my brothers were lying. But I couldn't just say that. The logic was on their side.

"I am sorry. It's just I am so tired of everything. Of people dying, and I just want them to stop dying. Especially on me."

"I know." Brother Reyansh spoke softly. "And I am sorry you have to go through all of this." We sat together in silence until lunch. My aunt Tulsi came in to call us for lunch. I was neither too close nor too distant with her. We were neutral. We talked when either she came over or when I went to her place. Mostly, I talked with Aunt Krishna. Aunt Tulsi was nice too. It was just that, I had known aunt Krishna my whole life, aunt Tulsi just got married with my uncle Kedar a few years ago.

"You boys, go and have lunch while I talk to your sister." She said putting up a smile. Her voice was honey sweet, and so were her words. She radiated warmth. And talking to her could relax anyone. Brothers Vihaan and Reyansh left and aunt Tulsi came to sit beside me.

"Look, honey. I know we aren't very close. But I want you to know, that you can always come and talk to me like you talk to your aunt Krishna. And know that your both brothers will always do what is good for you. Trust them to make some choices for you."

"What are you talking about?" I asked blankly.

"One day, soon, you'll know. Now, come on, let's have lunch." My uncle Kedar and aunt Tulsi had a daughter. So, Aunt

Tulsi went back to her home for the night, while my uncle Kedar, aunt Krishna and my cousin Vihaan had to stay back for thirteen days since they stayed the first night. My aunt Krishna's husband, uncle Sagar had gotten brother Vihaan's books for him and I and brother Reyansh were under strict orders from father to not disturb him. I went to school from the following Monday. Not everyone knew about my grandmother, just my close friends who I had texted from my laptop and my teachers. I sat on my place allotted by my class teacher. It was right in front of my best friend, Aheli, besides my competitor, Achal. Like I said before, I am the topper. Achal ranks up right after me, in second place. Most of the time, I score more than him. Sometimes, we tie. And very rarely, he scores more than me. We had a test today. A small one. Of 10 marks. But I knew I had to score more than Achal. I suddenly had a desire of winning; one I had never had before. It was a math test, so Achal had an advantage; most of the time, we tied in math test, and that was when I had studied hours before the test. Today, I had no chances of winning. Our first period was math and our teacher handed us our test papers. Achal completed before me and gave me a smug smile before handing the teacher his paper. I finished two minutes after him and then came back and started reading my history textbook. We were starting a new chapter in history today, and I hadn't studied over the weekend; so I had to at least read the chapter. After everyone finished their papers, ma'am gave us some sums and started checking our papers. We got our test results by the end of the class. Achal got his paper first. He had got a 9.5, and his face fell as soon as he read the numbers. He shot me a look of jealousy and put his paper inside his bag. Then I got mine. And I got my lowest marks ever in a 10 mark test. 8.75.

Those numbers were easy to make him grin.

"Aw, little girl need a tissue?" he asked slyly. I faced him, my face lightening up again. I went to my teacher and showed her the miscalculation. She had miscalculated and given me 8.75 instead of 9.75. I got back and resisted my urge to shove my paper in his face. I simply put it on my desk and he gave me a murderous look. The day went well. My history reading came handy when teacher asked general questions and I answered them all correctly. Suddenly I had the need to be in the spotlight. The teachers had thought that I would just stay quiet like I always do when something like this happens, but this time I didn't hide. I showed everyone I was the topper. There was no use of being one and just showing it in exams. The teachers liked me for my silence, so when everyone failed to answer, I volunteered, unlike the times when I knew but stayed quiet. Some teachers looked worried by this, while some appreciated it. By lunch time, I was already called by our class teacher to 'talk' and believe me, she seemed really worried. I don't know why, though. Isn't it good, I put myself out there? For me, it is. And I am starting to enjoy the attention I get.

After going home, I first completed my homework and went to the park. I live in a township, everything's here. Chemist, super market, park, even a school, the school I go to. Most of my friends stayed here too and so do some of my teachers. So, I have always had to be appropriate while going around here. I had brought a book to read and I sat on an empty park bench and started reading it. I read for around an hour and was stopped wen a softball hit me on my head. I turned to face a group of really young boys playing softball.

"Sorry," one of them yelled apologetically.

"it's alright, sweetheart." I said throwing the ball back at them. A lady, who looked around my brothers' age, appeared next to me.

Janushi Rajchura

VENTURES OF
GEM LAND
and the
Black Time
JANUSHI
RAICHURA

VENTURES OF
GEM LAND-2
The Gorgon's
Curse
JANUSHI
RAICHURA

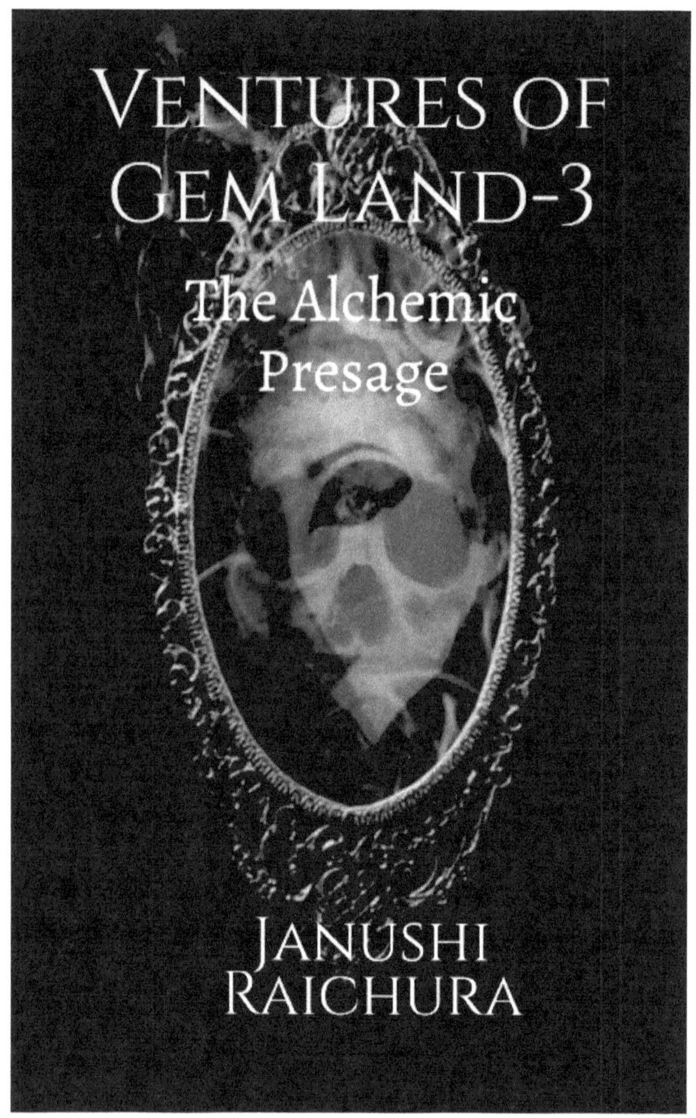

VENTURES OF
GEM LAND-3
The Alchemic
Presage
JANUSHI
RAICHURA

The Hues of
Samsara
Janushi Raichura

My Soul's
Verses
Janushi

Be A TWF
THE PRISMATIC
ELEVEN
Chief Editor
JANUSHI RAICHURA

VENTURES OF
GEM LAND
PART- 1, 2 AND 3
For the inevitable to approach, the first phase to
complete, the false child must decease.
JANUSHI
RAICHURA

87